Illustrated by the Disney Storybook Artists

A Random House PICTUREBACK® Book

Random House 🏠 New York

Copyright © 2002, 2010 Disney Enterprises, Inc. All rights reserved. Published in the United States by Random House Children's Books, a division of Random House, Inc., 1745 Broadway, New York, NY 10019, and in Canada by Random House of Canada Limited, Toronto, in conjunction with Disney Enterprises, Inc. Pictureback, Random House, and the Random House colophon are registered trademarks of Random House, Inc.

Library of Congress Control Number: 2002100493
ISBN: 978-0-7364-2065-5
www.randomhouse.com/kids
Printed in the United States of America
19 18 17 16 15 14 13 12 11 10

One stormy night, an old beggar woman went to the door of a castle. She offered the prince who lived there a rose in return for shelter. But the young man was horrified by her appearance and would not let her in.

Suddenly, the woman turned into a beautiful enchantress.

To punish the selfish prince, she changed him into an ugly beast and cast a spell over the castle and all who lived there. If the prince could learn to love and be loved in return before the last enchanted rose petal fell, then the terrible spell would be broken. If not, he would remain a beast forever.

In a nearby village lived a beautiful girl named Belle. Gaston the hunter wanted to marry Belle, but unlike all the other girls in the village, Belle didn't like him. She would rather read her books than listen to Gaston.

Belle's father, Maurice, was an inventor. One morning, he saddled up his faithful horse, Phillipe.

"Good-bye, Belle," said Maurice, kissing his daughter. "I'm off to the fair to show my latest invention."

But Maurice and Phillipe never made it to the fair.
They took a wrong turn and became lost in the dark
forest.

Suddenly, howling wolves startled Phillipe. The
terrified horse ran off, and Maurice fell from the saddle.

The inventor was barely able to escape the wolves!
He hid behind a castle gate.

Maurice stepped into the castle.

"Not a word," whispered Cogsworth, the clock, to Lumiere, the candlestick. The spell had transformed the servants into talking objects!

But the friendly Lumiere said, "Bonjour, monsieur!"

Maurice could not believe his eyes!

Suddenly, a huge beast stormed into the room. "Who are you? Why are you here?" he growled.

Before Cogsworth and Lumiere could explain, the Beast grabbed Maurice and threw him into the castle's dungeon.

When Phillipe arrived home without Maurice, Belle knew her father was in trouble. "You have to take me to him!" cried Belle.

They raced for the castle.

Once inside, Belle found her father locked in a cell.
They hugged through the bars as Maurice tried to explain
what had happened. But soon the Beast appeared.

Belle was frightened, but she pleaded with the Beast. "Please let my father go. Take me instead," she begged.

The Beast agreed. He threw Maurice out of the castle and then showed Belle to her room. "You can go anywhere you like . . . except the West Wing," he growled.

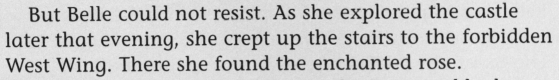

But Belle could not resist. As she explored the castle later that evening, she crept up the stairs to the forbidden West Wing. There she found the enchanted rose.

She was about to touch it when the Beast suddenly appeared! "Get out!" he shouted.

Terrified, Belle fled the castle and rode away on Phillipe.

Pairs of yellow eyes glowed in the dark forest as a pack
of wolves surrounded Belle and Phillipe.

Just as the animals were closing in, the Beast arrived.
He fought off the wolves and saved Belle.

Over time, Belle realized that the Beast had a good heart, and the two became friends. The Beast showed Belle his library, and Belle taught the Beast how to dance.

One day, after dancing in the ballroom, the Beast asked Belle if she was happy.

"Yes," Belle sighed. "If only I could see my father again."

The Beast brought Belle a magic mirror. In its reflection, she could see Maurice wandering in the forest, searching for her.

"You must go to him. Take the mirror with you so you'll always have a way to look back and remember me," said the Beast sadly.

Belle found her father and took him home. But their happiness did not last long. Gaston and a group of villagers soon learned about the Beast and set off for the castle to attack him.

When Belle found out, she fled back to the castle.
She found the Beast, but he was badly wounded.

Just as the last enchanted rose petal was about to
fall, Belle whispered, "I love you."

With those words, the Beast began to transform.
His claws turned into hands and his face grew smooth.
The spell was broken! He was human again!

Joyfully, all the enchanted objects in the castle returned to their human forms.

Love had saved the day. And Belle and her prince lived happily ever after.